Bud

"My Adventure Across America"

By Arthur Brood

Illustrated by Abby Killips

Cover Design by Amanda Karr

Dog Drawing for Chapters by Hannah Brood

Class Act Productions

www.classactproductions.us

Bud: My Adventure Across America

This story is based on actual events. Some characters and events have been added for dramatic effect.

For further information,
Contact Class Act Productions.

www.classactproductions.us

ISBN 978-0-9794851-5-2

My name is Bud, I am a bulldog with a tale to tell. Most dogs like to chase cars, and the car I chased made history. I was the first dog to ride across the country in a car way back in 1903. Here is how it happened.

My Journey

•••• This shows the part of the trip I did not travel and is not in my story.

⟶ This shows the part of the trip I traveled and is the story I am about to share with you.

 # Chapter 1

Excitement on Main Street

June 11th, 1903

I was just minding my own business, the same as any other dog, on that day in early June 1903. A heavy rainstorm was dumping water by the buckets, so I sought shelter under the front step of the blacksmith shop on Main Street of Caldwell, Idaho as Tom, my owner, ducked into the shop to get out of the sudden storm. The street had turned to mud, and the people that were caught in the downpour were sloshing across the street trying to get to a boardwalk where the muck would not stick to their boots. The windows in the shops were glowing with electric lights that sometimes flickered as the storm caused the electric lines to sway with each gale of wind. Suddenly, horses tied to hitching posts along the street started getting a bit jumpy and stomped their feet splashing mud with each stomp.

It was then I heard it, two quick blasts like someone playing a trombone in a marching band. My ears twitched as I tried to find where the sound came from. It was followed by a groaning, clattering noise mixed with a few squeaks that came from the west end of the street. It was clearly not a train, for no whistle had blown, and I had not heard the slight hum of the wheels on tracks, something only a dog can hear. Then I saw it! It was a carriage coming down the street! But wait! There was no horse pulling it! This is what was making all the noise. I shook my head and blinked my eyes in disbelief, I'd never seen anything like it in my life.

I got to my feet and left the shelter of the steps with a low growl in my throat. Something was wrong, since a carriage cannot move down the street without being pulled by a horse. I started barking to let Tom, my owner, know something was not right outside the shop. The carriage came splashing down the street and stopped in front of the hotel right across from me. Two men, who didn't seem at all concerned about losing their horse, got off the carriage. It was obvious they were on a long trip because the back of the carriage was piled high and covered with a tarp. The noise it made stopped, but all of a sudden a new smell drifted across the street. It stunk!

My barking alert must have worked better than I thought because people started coming out of several buildings and wading through the mud toward the visitors. A crowd started to swarm around the horseless carriage. The steady rain didn't bother them at all; they were curious about the strange carriage. Nobody asked about the missing horse or why it had made so much noise. Everyone was excited and were asking so many questions that the two men were having a difficult time answering all of them. In between bits of conversation I kept hearing a new word over and over again, MOTOR CAR.

Being a dog, it was easy for me to wiggle around and go between human legs to get a closer view of this mysterious machine that attracted the crowd. As I was the first dog on the scene, I took it upon myself to lift my rear leg by its rear wheel and be the first to claim this machine for myself.

Tom observed my behavior and immediately tried to call me back away from the carriage that I now knew was called a motor car. Normally I obey Tom right away, but my sense of curiosity was a little stronger. As he glanced away, I took the opportunity to walk under the motor car to investigate.

I was using my nose as all good dogs do. For us, it is like reading a newspaper because it tells us everything we need to know. As I sniffed around the strange motor car, I sensed an acidic smell near a pipe that ran the length of the bottom of the vehicle. I also smelled some oil near some very hot metal parts I later learned was the motor. I smelled a lot of strange smells that I did not recognize. I went about sniffing everything underneath to find as many answers as I could. The sudden introduction to such strong odors tickled my nose and caused me to sneeze. After three quick sneezes the tickling sensation was gone, and I licked the end of my nose and turned my attention to the gathering crowd.

The two visitors moved up onto the boardwalk to get shelter from the rain as they answered the hundreds of questions they were being asked by the small crowd that had gathered. A dog has a great ability to hear, so I was able to listen to more than one conversation at a time. Bending my right ear toward the conversation on the boardwalk I learned that the two men were trying to be the first to drive this motor car, which they also called an automobile, across the country, from San Francisco to New York City. I didn't know how far that was because I had never seen a map, but I assumed it must be pretty far because the men claimed they had already traveled 19 days and had made a bet it could be done in less than three months. I also learned they named this machine the "Vermont." I thought this was strange. I'd heard of people naming their horse, but who names their carriage?

After a while the crowd began to thin out. The visitors were given permission to store their machine, carriage, automobile, motor car, "Vermont", or whatever they called that crazy thing, at the stable next to the hotel to keep it out of the rain overnight. Tom whistled for me, I obediently trotted to his side, and we headed for home. I figured that the excitement was over, and I would never see the motor car again. Boy, I couldn't have been more wrong!

Chapter 2

My Life
Changes Forever

June 12th, 1903

I am not the only dog at Tom's home. I was born there in a litter of six pups a year earlier. We were a cute litter from what my mother told me. Most of us were tan and gray, but I was the only one that was tan and white. My heritage, of which I am proud, is that of a bulldog. As proud as I am of my heritage, it appears that the bulldog breed is not all that popular in small towns surrounded by ranch land. Herding dogs are the breed of choice, and so my brothers, sisters, and I were slow to be chosen for new homes. I was now a year old and the only pup left in the litter. My mother was not nearly as playful as my brothers and sisters, so I often went with Tom as he worked on his small farm outside of Caldwell.

The morning after my introduction to the new machine in town, I was chasing the chickens off the porch of the house when I heard a clattering sound coming from the road. I stopped, cocked my head a little to the left (I sometimes do that to make it look like I am listening really carefully) to investigate the sound I was hearing. The two men in the "Vermont" were bouncing down the road going a little faster than a horse at a trot. I leapt from the porch to give chase, sounding a long howl as I raced toward the road. I almost made it to the road when I heard the shrill whistle of Tom calling me back. So much for any fun this morning I thought to myself as I obediently trotted back to the house.

A short while later we, or maybe I should say Tom, was fixing a fence near the road. In all truthfulness, I was chasing prairie dogs. These squirrel-like creatures were easy to spot as they would stand straight up on their hind legs. They dug burrows in the ground that had multiple entrances, creating a challenge to the chase as they could go in one hole and pop out of another. They usually stuck together in small groups, so where there was one, there were many.

I had just chased a prairie dog around a boulder when I again heard the clattering sound that had only come from the motor car. This would be more exciting than chasing prairie dogs, so I let out a howl and bounded on to the road. Sure enough, the motor car was coming back toward town, and I gave chase. Tom began waving to the men driving, and they stopped the machine. They explained they had forgotten a coat at the hotel and were heading back to town to retrieve it.

Tom had noticed my keen interest in the motor car and asked the driver if he would like to have a mascot for his trip. The driver paused for a brief moment, looked at me, and told Tom he had been trying to find a dog to accompany them. A bulldog would make a perfect choice. He thought it might be helpful when they slept at night to keep wild animals away or to discourage robbers they might encounter; this was, after all, the Wild West. Tom knew I found too much mischief to stay on the farm; I needed room to roam. So after a few minutes, they struck a deal of $15, and my life changed forever.

Chapter 3

My Adventure Begins

I was coaxed to jump up on the car, which I willingly did, and sat at the feet of the two men. I was more than ready to leave the farm behind for the excitement of this new adventure, but I did give one last parting look at Tom to say a heartfelt goodbye.

I learned that the owner of the car was a gentleman who had made a bet he could drive across the country in three months. His name was Horatio Nelson Jackson. The other man was a mechanic named Seawell Crocker, who was hired to assist in repairing the car when it broke down and help with driving as needed. I soon learned how valuable Crocker was to our expedition because that horseless carriage, I came to know as the "Vermont," broke down many times.

After we had retrieved Jackson's coat from the hotel, we were on our way. I was so excited I could hardly contain myself. My tail was wagging so fast it was whipping the legs of the two men in the car.

We took roads that ran next to the railroad tracks, and I learned quickly that riding in the motor car was going to require learning new balancing skills as we bounced over the rough sections of roads. A few of the bigger bumps brought my jaw into hard contact with the cover over the front of the car. Luckily for me, I didn't have my tongue hanging out of my mouth, or I would have stabbed my tongue with my teeth. After a few miles, I put my front two paws on the dashboard which gave me a much better view of the road. This helped me see the rocks and holes that were obstacles in the road and allowed me to brace myself before we hit them.

When we came across a smooth section of road, Jackson increased the speed of the Vermont. The wind was blowing in my face as I rode with my front paws on the dashboard which dried out my mouth. My mouth was so dry that I couldn't even drool; that is rare for a bulldog. I longed for a drink of water.

We crested a hill and the car picked up even more speed. I had never gone so fast in my life; the wind was whistling in my ears and the landscape was blurring the sides of my vision. The wind was burning my eyes, which already were itchy from all of the dust. I was hoping we would not hit a large rock or other obstacle in the road; I was afraid I might be thrown off the Vermont which really was not an exciting thought at this rate of speed. I didn't want to die at such a young age in the middle of the desert.

The road transitioned back to going uphill, slowing the car, and we came to a spot where the road split and went in two directions. Jackson stopped the car and was studying his maps to make sure we were on the right road. I hopped down from the car and started rubbing my eyes to relieve the itching. Humans sure have it nice, being able to move their arms in different directions; the best that I was able to do was rub my eyes with the back of my paw. Crocker noticed my problem and pulled out a pair of extra goggles from his supplies. He adjusted the straps and fit them on my head and over my eyes. It felt funny at first, but I thought I would give them a try.

June 14th, 1903

In Nampa, Idaho Jackson was given directions to follow a set of railroad tracks. Traveling beside the railroad had some advantages. It was easy to follow our location on a map and we were sure to come across towns to get supplies that we would need. However, the biggest advantage was when we came across rivers that were too big to drive through.

Three hours into our journey we were stopped by such a river. I watched as Crocker got off the car and put his ear down on the railroad tracks. I was puzzled by this behavior, and tilted my head to the side. Crocker announced it was safe to cross and explained to Jackson he did not hear any sound of a train coming from the rails. Jackson then carefully drove the car onto the tracks. Although it was bumpy, we were soon across the river without getting wet. We repeated this many times over the next few weeks and rarely had to wait for a train.

Late in the afternoon, Jackson stopped the car. He said we should not be traveling so far south. He got out his maps and discovered that we were given the wrong directions in Nampa and had followed the wrong railroad tracks. This took us thirty-eight miles out of our way, and we turned around to get back on course. I had never been lost before, so I was feeling a little uneasy with my two traveling companions since we got lost on my first day. However, I was relieved to hear that we would be changing our direction of travel because the sun had been in my eyes all afternoon as we had driven south.

As the sun began to set in the western sky on my first day of travel with Jackson and Crocker, we had traveled only 45 miles from my home; however, we had spent 15 hours bouncing along in the motor car. All that traveling gave me an appetite, and I was given a piece of smoked meat and a slice of bread for dinner. Jackson and Crocker retrieved some blankets from their packed supplies, smoothed out the sand under the car and settled in for the night. I walked around in a few circles and settled down between the front wheels curled up with my nose touching my tail. Sleep did not come easy for me as I was very aware of my duties as night time security. Thankfully, nothing happened-- at least nothing that woke me up.

Chapter 4

Sick

June 15th, 1903

On my second day on board the Vermont, we came into the town of Mountain View. Crowds of curious people came to see us. I thought they came out to pet me, but I soon realized they had never seen a motor car and were more interested in the machine than the mascot who was covered in drool and dirt. I wanted to make sure to mark my territory on the rear wheel as soon as I jumped down so no other mongrels would try to claim the machine I had been entrusted to guard. I listened carefully to Jackson and Crocker talk about the car, and I soon learned why they called it the "Vermont." Apparently, Jackson lives in the state of Vermont. I guess he was a bit homesick and named the car with the same name. He does have some interesting quirks.

I would like to say that life couldn't have gotten any better than that, but I was wrong. Let me tell you!

I had started to get the hang of riding on the Vermont. I learned to brace myself for big bumps and lean when Jackson suddenly swerved to avoid a rock or hole in the road. However, I was not prepared for the next adventure. Over a small hill in the road, we suddenly came upon a big puddle. No, it was more like a pond. Crocker yelled out to hold on! How was I supposed to hold on? I have paws that are not like human hands, so I braced myself as we splashed into the water at a good speed. Water splashed over the front of the car as we came to a sudden stop. My goggles were intended to keep the dust out of my eyes, but I found they worked really well at keeping the water out too.

Jackson and Crocker seemed to be in a panic as they realized how deep the water was and that the Vermont was sinking deeper. Having only lived in a desert up to this point in my life, I had not had any experience swimming. I either had to learn quickly or drown. I leaped as far as I could for solid ground, and I discovered that instinct had already taught me how to swim. (Thankfully being a dog, instinct is part of our nature.) I started to dog paddle toward solid ground and was thankful to feel the mud squeeze between my toes as I pulled myself out and had a good shake to get the water off of me.

Jackson and Crocker were frantically trying to unload things off the motor car they wanted to keep dry. Jackson complained that for being in the desert, we sure were finding a lot of water. I could be of no assistance in this process and decided to take advantage of the water to get a much needed drink.

The water smelled and tasted a bit odd, but hey, I was so thirsty that I didn't care as I lapped up the water with my tongue. That was my mistake!

Jackson and Crocker were focused on getting the Vermont out of the mud hole. Boy, did they get it stuck. One of their tools, called a block and tackle, is a long rope with pulleys. One end of a rope is tied to a tree, a rock, or anything big that won't move. The rope then is looped around small pulley wheels and is attached to the Vermont's axle. The rope then pulls the Vermont out of the mud as it wraps around the axle. As hard as they worked, this method didn't work this time and they were getting pretty grouchy as nighttime settled in, and it started to rain. It looked like we would be stuck in the mud hole overnight.

Block and Tackle:
A rope attached to two pulleys that reduce the effort needed to pull a heavy object.

Meanwhile, my stomach started to ache. At first it started to gurgle, and then it started to cramp. I groaned in pain, and then all that water I had drunk came right back up my throat. Yuck! It tasted odd when I drank it, but it was disgusting when I threw it back up. It was a taste and smell I never want to experience again! Jackson, who just happened to be a doctor, looked me over and gave me some fresh water. He concluded I had drunk some water that had alkali in it. He explained that alkali, a substance found in the soil, just happened to mix with the water I had drunk. I learned that alkali was all over the place on our route through the western states. I also learned to trust my nose when I got a drink of water, and to never even think about lapping up water if it had the faintest smell of alkali.

Jackson and Crocker realized we were stuck, and that we would not be making any more progress for the day. Rather than attempting to pull the Vermont out in the rain, they made a makeshift tent out of their big coats and slept under them for the night. I was supposed to be on guard duty, but I was still feeling sick and slept the night away instead. Thankfully, any varmints looking for mischief kept away. Maybe they could smell the brave bulldog and kept their distance, or maybe the rain kept them all in their burrows. I think it was the bulldog, but Crocker thought it was the rain.

Chapter 5

Breakdowns

June 16th, 1903

The next morning while Jackson was checking me over to make sure I was back to full health (I would have acted sick longer if they would have given me scraps of meat for breakfast), Crocker started walking to find help. Luckily for him, help wasn't far away. A sheep herder used a horse to pull the "Vermont" out of the mud. In exchange for the help, Jackson gave the man a ride on the motor car. Ohhh was that funny to watch! The poor man started to panic and yell; apparently he had never gone that fast before. Crocker and I just watched and laughed.

We made it to Hailey, Idaho and were greeted much the same as in Mountain View. I was expecting a few more scratches behind the ears, but everyone seemed awed by the "Vermont." Jackson kept talking about needing to send a message by telegram for some parts for the car. He did that while we were in Hailey.

There were some strange things about Jackson. He liked to write, and every time we stopped, he wrote something. He wrote letters to his wife all the time and would send them by mail when we reached a town. He also kept very good records of every expense we had on our trip. I think he wrote in his sleep. Another odd thing about Jackson that I observed was when we had a break down or got stuck in a mud hole, he would often get out a small box and set it on a wooden stand. He would then fidget with the box. He claimed he was taking pictures, whatever that meant. Meanwhile, Crocker was left doing the hard work with the car.

Shortly after leaving Hailey, Idaho, we traveled through some strange land. Solid black rock covered the ground and there were no flat surfaces, just rough rock. Only a few plants were able to find a crack in the rock to set roots and grow. Jackson and Crocker had to carefully steer the "Vermont" around this rough terrain. I overheard them say it was a lava flow. I still have no clue what a lava flow is, but I know it was a solid surface on which we didn't get stuck. The lava flow may have been solid, but I am not sure we made much better time as we snaked around trying to find a path the car could drive on.

Once the lava flow was behind us, we came across a portion of road that was smoother, and Jackson was able to make the car go faster. We were going so fast the wind was howling past my ears and the landscape was blurring in my eyes, but I didn't dare close them. If I closed my eyes for one brief moment, we might hit something in the road that would knock me down and slap my jaw on the front of the car again. I already learned that lesson, and I didn't want to do it again.

As the sun was setting behind us, we came into a small town called Soda

Springs. Crocker gave the horn a toot that sounded like a fog horn to announce our arrival. I wish he would have told me before he did that; it startled me and is rather hard on a dog's ears. We sped down the main street of town and puttered to a stop in front of a hotel.

I was starting to get used to a crowd gathering every time we stopped in a town, but I usually retreated to hide under the car. This crowd was quite a mix of cowboys, sheepherders, and Native Americans. A loud "whoop" passed down the street to show their approval of our arrival in the motor car.

I slept under the car that night—well, tried to sleep. There was a big fight that spilled out of the neighboring saloon that kept me on edge until sometime in the middle of the night.

I was awakened by a gentle nudge from the toe of Crocker's boot before the rooster crowed for the sunrise. Jackson wanted to be on the road again before the sun was up. Didn't he know I was up half the night guarding the car? I yawned and stretched before hopping up on the car. We weren't far down the road when I heard a strange groaning and grinding sound from the front of the car. I looked back at Crocker who did not seem concerned at all. I guess it was one of those sounds only a dog can hear. I nudged his leg with my nose and gave a groan as a signal, but his response was to reach down and scratch my head between my ears, telling me he didn't get much sleep either. I greatly enjoy my head being scratched, but this was not a time for enjoyment; something was not right with the car.

A few more miles and that groaning sound was getting so loud I wanted to put my paws over my ears, but then Crocker told Jackson to stop the car. I have learned that when Crocker told Jackson to stop the car, it was going to be a while before we moved again as something was usually broken. As the car came to a stop, I

hopped down and did a quick sniff of
the area to make sure this was a safe
place for Jackson and Crocker. This was
just part of my job as the security
guard. Convinced it was safe and that
we would be there for awhile, I
retreated to the shade under the car. I
didn't see the sense in staying in the
blazing sun because dogs don't sweat;
we pant. Panting in a dusty desert is
not my idea of fun.

It turned out the groaning sound
was a pretty big deal. Crocker said the
front bearing and hub on the wheel
were no good. Crocker went off to find
help or parts as Jackson and I stayed
with the car. I jumped up on a boulder
and watched him walk away, whining
my protest to Jackson who did not
seem to be bothered much at all. Well,
it bothered me! I did not like it at all
when one of them wandered off alone.

To take my mind off of Crocker's
absence, I started snooping around and
found the bones of a dead antelope.
Grabbing a leg bone, I spent a good

portion of the day gnawing on the bone to pass the time. It was a bit dry, but it gave me something to do. Anyway, all dogs like a good bone once in awhile.

It took all day to repair the car with the help of a local farmer who had let Crocker take bearings from his mowing machine. Crocker was good at fixing the "Vermont," but he didn't have all the tools to make this repair. He enlisted the help of a local blacksmith, and by late evening, they had performed the needed repairs.

It was too late in the day to start traveling, so Jackson and Crocker spent the night in a hotel in Montpelier, Idaho while I spent the night under the car as was my habit. My job as security was around the clock. A stray cat was poking around looking to jump up on the Vermont. I solved its prowling mischief with a low growl that sent it scampering away. Other than that, nothing exciting happened.

On the road again the next day, we finally crossed into Wyoming.

Jackson was convinced the worst was behind us and told Crocker we were going to cross a lot of miles today. He spoke too soon. I started hearing that groaning and grinding sound from the front of the car again, and I had my doubts. Jackson and Crocker soon figured it out, too. Crocker told Jackson we would go easy to see if we could make it to another town. I chose to walk beside the car as I did not have to worry about being left behind. The broken bearing caused the car to go so slowly a turtle would have been able to pass it.

After what seemed like forever, we came across another town of sorts. There were structures, but it didn't look like any of the towns we had visited up to this point. This was a mining town, and we stopped at the mine office. It had big buildings up on stilts with railroad tracks coming in and out. There were only men there, and most of them looked pretty dirty, I guessed because of the small mountains of coal that they were piling up.

Although the goggles had been a big help, my eyes were hurting because of the alkali dust from the road. The deafening noises of the mining machinery was limiting my range of hearing, and the numerous smells that go with a factory were challenging my sniffer. All I wanted was a long nap.

Crocker said this town was a bit of good luck. A man at the mine had special skills in making parts, which was his job, and would be able to make a new part for us. Good luck for them maybe, but for me it was terrible not being able to hear or smell well due to the noise and dust of this place. It really put my security skills to the test! We slept on the floor of the machine shop overnight and repairs were made the next morning. Jackson gave several rides in the "Vermont" to those who helped us with repairs, and by afternoon we were on the road again. I was glad to be leaving!

 # Chapter 6

Stuck in a Mud Hole

June 19th, 1903

I took my usual perch with my front paws on the dashboard as I sat between Jackson and Crocker's feet. From this vantage point I could see the road ahead, and I was somewhat safe from being jostled off the motor car on rough roads. I used my position to scan the road ahead for obstacles that might be dangerous such as rocks or mud holes. I would alert Jackson and Crocker with two short "woofs" if I saw something in the road. After a while I had them trained, and they slowed down when I gave them the signal.

As we approached a small stream, Jackson brought the car to a stop. I leaped to the ground, took a customary sneeze to clean out my sniffer, and waded into the cool water. I had to make sure the water was safe for drinking. When it passed my sniffer test, I proceeded to lap it up with my long tongue. Jackson and Crocker took off their boots, rolled up their pant legs and also waded out into the creek. They were surprised to find the creek bed was quite firm in the shallow water and decided it might be easier to drive the car in the creek bed instead of on the rough road that ran beside it. For the next half hour, I sprinted up and down the stream with puppy like energy as water from the stream splashed in all directions. The refreshing water was a pleasant change from the dry dust of the past few days. This was much more fun than riding on the Vermont.

Meanwhile, Jackson and Crocker, aboard the Vermont, plodded steadily onward. When the stream approached the entrance to a canyon, Crocker suggested it would be a good idea to get back on the road. He did not know what lay ahead in the canyon and did not want to be in there if we should encounter another rainstorm. Although I wanted to continue splashing in the water, I also didn't want to be left behind. I reluctantly left the stream and gave Jackson and Crocker a good shower when I shook myself dry.

It was getting close to dark and was at the stage of twilight when there is just enough light to sort of see things but not enough light to create shadows to see things clearly. Crocker had not yet lit the big headlight in the center of the front of the car. My goggles were smeared from my drool splashing back on them, so my keen eyes were straining to see in the twilight when all of a sudden there was a big splash and we jolted to a stop. The abrupt stop caused me to slide up onto the hood. Fortunately a spare tire was strapped to the front of the car that kept me from sliding into the drink. I have no idea how we didn't see this huge mud hole sitting in the middle of the road.

In situations like this, Crocker usually got off the car, took off his coat and shirt to keep them dry, and then reached down into the muddy water to wrap one end of the rope connected to the block and tackle around the rear axle. Jackson would drag the other end of rope to something large like a tree or boulder. Crocker would then put the car in gear, and the car would pull itself out as the rope wrapped around the rear axle. Not this time. First of all, the car motor sputtered and then quit when we landed in the mud hole. Crocker tried and tried, but it refused to start again. Making matters worse, there were no trees or boulders to attach the other end of the block and tackle. To add to our misery, we were wet and nighttime was setting in.

Jackson started off on foot to find help, and I started to tag along, I mean it was my job as security. Jackson commanded me to stay. I tilted my head and whined, but in the end I just watched him walk away. Meanwhile, Crocker had waded back into the mud hole and discovered the batteries were all wet which was what was keeping the car from starting.

I needed something to do to keep my mind off of Jackson wandering aimlessly in the dark in an unknown desert without me to protect him. Realizing there was nothing I could do to help Crocker, I decided to stretch my legs. Night time is when the jack rabbits come out, and being a young dog, I had lots of energy for chasing them.

Jack rabbits are hard to catch. They have very large ears with incredible hearing so there is not a good way to sneak up on them. However, those large ears were also quite easy for me to see as they go up like flags. My advantage was that the rabbits were curious about what Crocker was doing in the mud hole, which is where they wanted to get their drink. I would lay down in a crouched position behind some sage brush and wait until I saw the ears on a jack rabbit go straight up and twitch as it listened to Crocker. I would then leap up and the chase was on. Those little rascals were good at this game and would run zigzag, make circles around rocky outcroppings, and dive in holes only to reappear out of another hole, not to mention they were fast. I never did catch one. After a few hours, I felt well exercised, so I plopped down on a sandy knoll and watched Crocker as he tinkered with the car.

I was starting to get quite concerned about Jackson as he had left to find help at dusk. It was now well into the middle of the night, and Jackson still had not returned. Around three a.m. the stillness of the night was interrupted by the steady sound of horse hooves and a few muffled voices in the distance. I gave a low growl to warn Crocker something was not right before I launched into my warning barks to let our approaching visitor know I would protect Crocker at all costs. I was answered with a shrill whistle that I immediately recognized belonged to Jackson. He then called my name, and I forgot all about Crocker and took off to meet Jackson. He had walked 13 miles before he found someone with a horse willing to come help in the middle of the night. He had to be exhausted from all the walking, but his relief of finding us renewed his energy. In no time at all, the car was pulled up onto dry ground.

Relieved that Jackson was safely back, I dozed in and out over the next several hours. I don't think Jackson or Crocker got much sleep as they were pretty concerned about getting the batteries dried out. About 9 a.m. we were back on the road.

Chapter 7

We Get Lost

June 20th, 1903

June 20th, 1903

We had just passed through Granger, Wyoming when another huge thunderstorm rolled through and washed out the road we were traveling on so that it was impassable. Seeing the car did not have a top, we were drenched to the skin. Being a dog, I just shook the water off. Jackson and Crocker did not appreciate the extra shower and threatened to throw me out of the car. One benefit of the rain was that I always took it upon myself to stick out my tongue and lick up the fresh water falling from the sky because it was safer than drinking out of some of those puddles. This area is known for its dry climate, but it sure rained a lot as we traveled through.

When the cloudburst let up, Jackson took out his map and thought we could go cross country without any roads since the road ahead of us had washed out. Using his compass and the map, he directed us in a generally eastward direction without a road. There were many hills to cross; I would learn these were called mesas and buttes. They have steep sides, sometimes straight up and down, but have flat tops. It was hard to believe that the Vermont could drive up and over all but the steepest. Jackson called this area the badlands of Wyoming, and we soon found out why.

My skills of balance were being put to a new test in my lookout position as we very slowly navigated around rocks, sage brush and up and down ravines and slopes of mesas. The car rocked from side to side and sometimes felt as if it might tip over as we drove along the banks of some steeper ravines. When I leaned to the right, the car lurched to the left, so for my safety I chose to just trot beside the car. My fear of getting tossed from the car was greater than my fear of getting left behind. I knew they couldn't travel faster than I could run.

This was typically a dry climate, and the water quickly disappeared from these ravines despite the sudden thunderstorms. However, the lack of grass to hold the soil together meant the gravelly sand was loose and difficult to drive through, resulting in the car becoming stuck more times than I could count. At first, Crocker tried tying ropes around the rear wheels to give the car better traction. Even though that helped some, they eventually started cutting sage brush and laying it down in front of the wheels for a hundred feet at a time to keep the car from sinking in the soft ground. They would then stop, get the brush they just drove over and return it to the front of the car to drive another hundred feet.

I thought it was a game and sometimes took the sagebrush before it was ready to be moved. After trying to keep it away from Jackson and Crocker, I realized they weren't very interested in playing this game and threatened to tie me to the car. The threat of being tied up was a clear enough warning, so I gave up and just tagged along chasing the little lizards that were darting from one rock to another.

All of a sudden I heard a rattling sound next to Crocker. A rattlesnake was coiled and ready to strike him. I lunged at the snake taking its focus off Crocker's leg. The snake snapped at me, but I darted out of danger. I was barking and growling, but the snake wasn't backing down. I had caught garter snakes, but my mother had warned me not to mess with a rattlesnake. Now I could see why. In the midst of all the excitement I heard a huge BANG! Jackson was right behind me holding a rifle with smoke drifting out of its barrel. The snake lay still on the ground. If it wasn't for my excellent hearing and quick reflexes, Crocker would have been in a heap of trouble. After a few moments to let the intensity of the moment subside, he reached down and scratched me between the ears praising me for saving his life.

After several hours on our cross country course, even Jackson admitted we were hopelessly lost as we zigzagged through the barren Wyoming country. However, I knew we must be close to something as the scent in the wind started to change. About that same time the landscape began to level out, and we were on a gentle downward slope that suddenly dropped and gave us a view of the Green River.

A bigger challenge was now before us. How to get across? When it was a small stream we would drive through it. On larger rivers we crossed on railroad bridges. The Green River was much too deep to drive across, and we had lost sight of the railroad.

As Jackson again studied his maps and compass, I went down to the river. Now that I knew I could swim, I found a cool dip in a river was quite refreshing. Even though I am not too particular about how clean I am, I do need a good bath once in a while. I was enjoying the refreshing dip when I felt something nibble on the end of my tail.

Startled, I lunged for the shallower water. I then turned around to find that several small fish were darting around me and thought my tail must be their lunch. This made me a bit uneasy, so I thought it was best to get out of the water even though it felt so good.

Returning back to the car Jackson had decided we should follow the river to the south. That evening it was discovered that during our journey through the rough terrain earlier in the day, all of the food and cooking utensils had fallen off the car. Jackson and Crocker were both upset at themselves for not securing the load more securely. A rumble in my stomach told me we were going to bed hungry.

I remembered the fish that had nibbled on my tail while swimming in the river earlier in the evening. I thought if there are little fish then there must be big fish too, and they might make a meal. I whined and tilted my head to the side as I tried to convince Jackson and Crocker to come to the river to catch a fish, but they just told me they were as hungry as I was and ignored me. How come people cannot understand dogs as well as we dogs can understand people?

After the intense journey of the last two days and the lack of sleep the previous night, Jackson and Crocker settled in for a night of sleep despite their hunger. I, on the other hand, was not so quick to fall asleep. The sounds of animals and insects that live by rivers were new to me. This was my first introduction to mosquitos. There had to be thousands of them, and the sound of their buzzing around my ears and biting my back had me restless all night. I was also introduced to the chorus of hundreds of frogs on the banks of the river.

These new sounds really were confusing my ability to stay alert for any danger that might be approaching our little camp. Of bigger concern to me was a comment Crocker made when they were unable to locate any food. As fond of my protective services as they were, he mentioned that if they were not able to find food soon they might be forced to eat roasted bulldog. How can one sleep knowing you might be tomorrow's main dish?

Chapter 8

Help When
We Needed It

June 22nd, 1903

It was a beautiful sunrise as the sun rose over the towering bluffs along the Green River. I awakened before Jackson or Crocker, having kept my senses on high alert after their conversation the evening before about roast bulldog. I snuck quietly out of our campsite. If I could find a prairie dog den, I could bring back a meal and save my neck. Prairie dogs are not as fast as jack rabbits and there are a lot of them. However, they are tricky to catch as they work as a team. They rarely travel away from their burrows alone and one is always on guard. They also have multiple entrances to their burrows and can dive into a hole in the ground a casual observer may never see. Also, when one is being chased, the whole family comes out and starts making whistling sounds which distracts the pursuit. So they are difficult to catch but not impossible, especially when your life is on the line. Unfortunately for me, those prairie dogs were sleeping in, and I trotted back to camp without a hint of breakfast.

Jackson and Crocker were up and were relieved that I came trotting back. I will never know if their relief was because I was the security team or potential breakfast. The car was soon loaded and we started on our day. Jackson decided we should continue to follow the river south hoping to find a town or the railroad.

Around midday, I noticed something that didn't quite fit the landscape. There was a large mass of grayish white, but parts of it appeared to move. Due to the car bouncing over the rough terrain, I could not focus my gaze on it clearly. I put my nose to the wind, but the wind was coming from behind us, and all I could smell was the exhaust from the car. I perked up my ears, but the puttering of the motor and the sound of the wheels crunching over the gravel and sage brush covered any other sounds. I barked my signal "woof woof" to alert Jackson and Crocker that something ahead was different and to be watchful.

As we got closer it became apparent that it was a large herd of sheep. Jackson and Crocker became very excited, and I licked my lips. A lonely sheepherder, holding his rifle ready, cautiously greeted us. He had heard the Vermont puttering, but did not see a horse pulling it. When he saw me he raised his rifle slightly in my direction and told Jackson and Crocker that if I went after his flock of sheep, he would have no choice but to shoot me. I got the message and answered with a low growl.

Jackson enthusiastically greeted the startled fellow and begged for some food. After a brief explanation describing the car and our adventures of the last few days, the man relaxed and invited us to a meal of roast lamb.

The man tossed me a used corncob to chew on; apparently he thought this would distract any interest I might have in chasing his sheep. He didn't have to worry about me. If he was going to prepare a meal, I had no interest in chasing his sheep. At that moment an odd thought crossed my mind-- here I was a "bull" dog, and I was enjoying a lamb dinner.

Jackson learned that the man had not seen another person in 3 weeks and was quite startled when he saw us riding on the Vermont. We also learned that if we headed due south, away from the river, we would again find the railroad which would lead us to a town. Jackson offered to pay the man, which he refused, but in the end he accepted one of our two rifles as a token of our great appreciation.

The tension of finding food was now passed, and I was able to once again relax as I perched in my usual spot with my feet on the dashboard watching the route ahead. After two hours we came upon the railroad, and Jackson turned the car east.

Crossing a small creek, the car became stuck trying to climb the sand bank on the other side. Jackson and Crocker got out the shovel and started digging. Dogs are excellent diggers, so I thought I could be of some help. I guess I was a bit ambitious as Crocker complained about getting a face full of flying sand.

We spent the better part of two hours digging sand away from the car when I sensed approaching visitors. I let out a low growl and found a high point on the bank to get a better view. Sure enough, three men carrying large bundles on their backs were approaching. I let out my warning barks, and Jackson came over to see what was troubling me.

Jackson had a magical way with people. He convinced these three young men to help us get the car out of the sand. In exchange, Jackson offered to carry their bags on the car to the next town. I encouraged the men by barking at their heels as they pushed the car up the sand bank and on to solid ground. We loaded up our new baggage and were on our way.

Chapter 9

Be Careful
Whom You Meet

We again approached the banks of the Green River. The little town of Bitter Springs on the nearby bank was a welcome sight. When we drove into town, I think Jackson was feeling the pressure of being behind, since he spent little time with the curious crowds that gathered. I was left to guard the car. A little growl from a bulldog kept most curious onlookers from getting too close. Meanwhile, Crocker went to get supplies while Jackson dropped off the men's baggage at the Bitter Creek train depot and checked on the train schedule to make sure it was safe to cross the bridge.

When the errands were done, Jackson drove the car to the train tracks near the railroad bridge. Crocker put his ear down on the rail and listened for any vibrations that might indicate an approaching train. Satisfied it was safe to cross, Jackson drove the car onto the rails. The rails just fit between our wheels, and we started driving down the tracks. It was a bit bumpy as the railroad ties didn't create a very smooth surface, but it was a way across the river that didn't involve getting wet. I stayed on extra high alert as I didn't trust Crocker's method of knowing if a train was coming. If a train was coming, I was going to jump from the car. The ground started to drop away as the tracks started to rise into the air as we drove onto the railroad bridge. A few moments later we were about 50 feet above the water. I looked around and thought that this must be what it felt like to be a bird. I took my paws off the dashboard. I needed to make sure I was a little bit more stable in case something happened. I didn't like the idea of falling from the sky.

Once we crossed the bridge, we drove beside the railroad and not on it. Jackson said we wouldn't get stuck in mud or sand if we stayed on the tracks, but there was a risk of meeting trains. He felt that the chance of not being able to get off the tracks for an approaching train would certainly bring our trip to an early end.

As we approached the small town of Rock Springs, I saw a long colorful train parked along the tracks. The town also seemed to be a beehive of activity, and a very large tent was being set up. As we drove into town, Jackson honked the horn, and the normal crowd of people swarmed the car. Jackson was asked if he was part of the circus, to which he replied that he was not part of the circus but was driving an automobile across the country.

My sniffer was sensing a smell I had never smelled before, so I hopped off to investigate. As I weaved through the maze of human legs with my sniffer to the ground, I was getting a very strong scent of an animal I didn't recognize. Just then I came across what looked like the trunks of four large trees. As I stopped and looked up, one of the trees lifted right out of the ground, and I found out it was not a tree. A very large animal was before me; one step from his foot would squish me, so I scampered out of the direction it was walking.

As I tilted my head to the side in curiosity and looked at this large beast, a large hose attached to the front of its head swung close to my face. I was frozen in surprise when I quickly realized the large hose was his nose, and he sniffed me like I have never been sniffed before. It let out a gentle rumbling sound, and I realized that it wanted to be friends. At that moment the person holding the rope nearby yelled to get that dog away from the elephant, and I was shooed away. So in a brief moment, I learned that this large creature was an elephant and that we would never meet again, much to my disappointment. It never hurts to have a friend that is bigger than you.

My nose also told me there was a cat nearby. I never miss an opportunity to chase a cat. Putting my sniffer to work once again, I followed the scent which led me to a large crate on a small wagon. I jumped up on the front of the wagon to surprise the cat that my nose told me was hiding by the crate. As I crested the side of the wagon, I was greeted by the fiercest roar I have ever heard in my life, and a paw half the size of my head swung at me through the cage door just missing my whiskers. I fell off the wagon backwards and bolted for the safety of the crowd near Jackson and Crocker. I might be in charge of security on our trip, but that cat would have had me for lunch. I had never seen a cat that big. I later learned it was called a lion, and I had nightmares for the next few days as I relived my very brief encounter with it. Now when I smell a cat, I double check its size before I get too close.

Jackson was not interested in staying for the circus, and I was not sure I wanted to meet any more new animals. A few minutes after I returned to the car, we were safely on our way and racing for Rawling, Wyoming.

Chapter 10

Unexpected Delay

Racing may have been a bit optimistic. On a good road we might be able to go 25 to 30 miles per hour, on a bad road a walking pace would feel fast. Often, I would hop off and trot beside the car when the pace became too slow.

The rains over the past week had stopped, and instead of the threat of mud holes, we were faced with the threat of sand holes. Just before nightfall we found a deep one. After all the digging earlier in the day, Jackson and Crocker decided to set up camp and try digging out in the morning.

I was becoming well trained in digging. Both of my front paws could send sand flying at a faster rate than Jackson or Crocker with their shovel. I tried to show them again how easy it was, but they weren't very good at digging with their hands.

Crocker was a genius at finding a way to get the car out of whatever situation we found ourselves stuck in. He had acquired an anchor at some point that he attached to the end of the rope with the block and tackle. When there was not a tree or rock available, he dug the anchor down into the ground to help us pull the car from the mud or sand. After a short while Jackson and Crocker had the car back on solid ground. We reloaded everything we had taken off of the car and were back on our way.

June 23rd, 1903

As we came into Rawlings, Wyoming, Jackson announced our arrival by honking the horn. I wish he wouldn't have done that as it startled me every time we entered a town. I was so alarmed that I almost jumped out of the car each time. We were once again greeted by a crowd of curious spectators. They were especially amused by the goggles I wore to protect my eyes from all the dust. I rubbed my head against Crocker's leg, and he took them off for me.

Jackson and Crocker thought this town would be a good place to get a hotel and get cleaned and rested up after several nights of sleeping under the stars. Hey, dogs sleep on the ground all the time, so I didn't see what the big deal was all about.

As Crocker drove the car to park it for the night, a terrible noise clanked from the motor and the car came to a sudden stop. Crocker quickly identified a major problem, and Jackson had to order parts from the factory. This meant we stayed in Rawlings for almost a week instead of one night.

Being a visitor in the community, I took it upon myself to do a little socializing, but the other dogs only looked at me from a distance. They were herding dogs. Since I was a bulldog, we didn't have much in common. To pass the time I thought I could show them that I could chase animals just as well as they could. A stray cat was lurking behind a barrel, and I let out a howl and gave chase which made the herding dogs despise me even more. One old border collie snarled that any dog can chase a cat but to herd livestock takes special skills.

Seeing my own kind chose not to befriend me, I went searching for a boy. Before I joined Jackson and Crocker, I had found that young boys would always play with me. Behind the general store I noticed one boy that was limping and was not able to play with the other boys.

I picked up a rock I was able to carry in my mouth and dropped it beside him and started licking his swollen ankle. He giggled from my lickings. I nudged the rock with my nose to give him a hint I wanted to play. He picked it up and threw it to the edge of a fence. I bounded after it, beginning a fun game of fetch. The three other boys stopped what they were playing and thought it was great fun to chase me, so I played keep away, but I always dropped the rock at the hurt boy's feet for him to throw. I learned his name was Sam, and I spent a lot of time with him that week. Apparently his father owned the general store, because he would sometimes go in and come back out with treats for me -- a nice bonus I had not planned on. Sam asked if he could keep me, but his father knew I belonged to Jackson and that I would need to stay with him.

The repairs on the Vermont were nearly finished, and I knew we would be leaving early the next morning. I had enjoyed my time with Sam, but I knew my place was with Jackson and Crocker. Sam was gently stroking my back with tears in his eyes as he said goodbye. I wanted to let him know I would also miss him. The only thing I could think to do was to lick him across his tear stained face with all my dog slobber. He smiled as he gave me one last pat.

Chapter 11

On the Road Again

June 28th, 1903

After the fifth day, the car was repaired and we were ready to resume our journey. Jackson and Crocker got on the car and whistled for me to jump up. However, they had not put on my goggles yet, and I was not leaving until they did. I whined and rubbed my paw over my eyes which reminded them about my goggles. I had them trained well. Once the goggles were on, I jumped up and took my place proudly in the center of the car. Sam came over and giggled as I licked his face good bye. I enjoyed my time with him, but it was time to be on our way.

The road began to change from sandy trails, in which the Vermont had struggled to find traction, to rocky trails on the steep slopes of Elk Mountain. The car barely had enough power to push itself up the steep inclines. I often got off and trotted beside the car. Sometimes we had to stop altogether and push big boulders out of the road; at other times we had to get out the block and tackle to pull the car over some steep sections of the trail. On one day they used the block and tackle seventeen times.

Through this new terrain I was not able to help as much. My paws are good for digging in sand, but I can't move rocks and stones very easily. When we stopped, I entertained myself by chasing little ground animals called marmots, which were similar to overgrown prairie dogs. These fat little creatures were much slower than and not nearly as smart as prairie dogs, so they were fairly easy to catch. They made an interesting whistling sound which helped me find them quickly. I would catch one and proudly carry it by the scruff of its neck back to Jackson and Crocker. We weren't in need of food at this time, so I let the little creatures go once Jackson and Crocker saw my prize catch.

July 1st, 1903

I had only been with Jackson and Crocker for about three weeks, but I had a lifetime of travel. Now, off Elk Mountain, Jackson sped the car up on the smooth road that lay ahead. I had no idea the car could go so fast. For a while we were almost keeping up with the train that was on the track beside the road. People were sticking their heads out the window to get a good look at us. Jackson finally slowed us down because the smoke from the coal powered train engine was blowing in our face and smelled really bad.

As we approached Cheyenne, Wyoming, I prepared for Jackson's traditional honk of horn. I figured if I pointed my head the opposite direction of the horn it might not hurt my ears as badly. It helped, but I still jumped when he squeezed the bulb which let off the noisy blast from the horn.

People that were on the train must have announced our upcoming arrival. Crowds had gathered, and they were calling the car the "Whiz Wagon" because it had gone so fast when traveling beside the train.

The people in Cheyenne were excited to see us. Reporters from the newspaper crowded around us, and I had to give a little growl and show my teeth to get people to back up so I had room to jump down and take my place under the car. It was safer there; people couldn't step on me. It was also a sign of things to come. The more progress we made on our journey the more reporters became interested in making us front page news.

Chapter 12

Playing in the Snow

July 2nd, 1903

We only stayed in Cheyenne overnight. The next morning I again took my place on the car as we headed east out of town. It turned out to be a short day of travel as an hour out of town a terrible noise came from the motor, and we again came to a stop. I was beginning to think I could walk across the country faster than riding in this car that broke down so often. Fortunately for us we were still beside the railroad. A railroad crew towed the car back to their work camp where Crocker started working on the car. Jackson ordered more parts, and we waited again for the parts to arrive.

Staying at the railroad camp was more exciting than being stranded in a big town. The men of the camp would throw sticks for me to chase, and I had room to stretch my legs with a good run. Although not in the mountains anymore, we were still in high elevations. On our third day at the camp it started to snow. Being that it was supposed to be summer it wasn't a big snowstorm. I started chasing some of the larger snowflakes thinking this was great fun. Pretty soon enough snow had fallen to make snowballs, and one of the men started throwing them to me. I would try to catch them, sometimes tumbling to the ground with what was left of one of the snowballs. The fun came quickly to an end when the short snowstorm ended as quickly as it began, and the snow began melting on the warm ground.

Jackson was amazed at the snow in July and asked if this was common. The men shared with him that it had been the wettest summer in memory and that there had been numerous storms, so snow was not too much of a surprise. Jackson explained that we were well aware of how wet the summer was as we had been stuck in countless mud holes, even though we were in the desert.

July 7th, 1903

The car was again repaired, and we were on our way after saying goodbye to our new friends at the railroad camp. The path ahead appeared to be some of the best terrain I had seen since starting this trip. The tall mountains were behind us, and the land was mostly flat with some gentle hills popping up here and there. The sand of the desert and the rocks of the mountains were replaced with green grasslands that stretched as far as my eyes could see. I had only known mountains and arid desert up to this time. My nose was sensing the aroma of grasslands, a scent I did not yet recognize. I stood as tall as I could with my paws on the hood of the car and eagerly anticipated what lay before us.

Chapter 13

The Prairie

Although the land was flat, the tall grass made it a little more difficult to see things around us. I began using my nose a little more, and one day I smelled a horse, even though I could not see it. I let out my howl of warning. All of a sudden we came across a farmer and his wife in a wagon pulled by the horse I had smelled. The farmer was so startled by us in the car that he quickly cut his horse loose from the wagon, and he and his wife dove underneath the wagon trying to hide from us. Jackson and Crocker roared with laughter at the sight. Despite trying to convince the poor farmer that the car was harmless, he was not convinced. After a few minutes, we proceeded on our journey.

The summer rainstorms continued, but unlike the desert where much of the water quickly absorbed into the ground, or the mountains where it quickly flowed into gullies or ravines, the rainwater on the prairie just stayed there making mud. I spent a lot of time walking, but I could rarely enjoy it because the mud was squishing between my toes. This also meant that Jackson got the car stuck many times. He now called the mud holes, "Buffalo Wallows". They seemed like the same thing to me, a small pond of water that would stop the car and cause me to take an unwanted swim.

The tall grass made it very difficult for me to see when I was on the ground. It was like a jungle to me with grass towering far above my head and growing so thick I had to push to get through it. Chasing little ground critters, like mice and snakes, had become more difficult as the grass would trip me when I tried to run. However, a new form of entertainment came my way. Grasshoppers!

We came across several miles where the tall grass had thinned so much I could see quite a distance and trot easily beside the car. All of a sudden a bunch of grasshoppers started jumping up. These were fun to chase and I leaped after them and would snap at them. I found them to be quite tasty and figured I would eat as many as I could, seeing Jackson and Crocker had a habit of running short on food.

The further we drove, the more abundant these grasshoppers became. There were thousands, no millions, of them. They were so thick at times that they looked like a cloud in the sky. This of course made it easy for me to pounce and grab a snack. I could even snatch them out of the air while riding on the car. After a couple hours of this game, my stomach started feeling funny. When the car again became stuck, I got off and laid down beside it. The next thing I knew, all those grasshoppers I had eaten came back up as I threw up the carcasses of hundreds of grasshoppers. Crocker just laughed and said I learned my lesson. I don't think I will ever eat another grasshopper as long as I live.

We were all getting tired of mud holes, buffalo wallows, or whatever they called them here. Jackson decided he would make a detour to find ground that was more suitable for driving. Even if the distance was longer, he thought we could save time rather than continually dig the car from the mud.

As we progressed on our journey, we crossed several more rivers on train bridges. As usual, Crocker put his ear to the track to check for a train before driving the car onto the bridge. At one bridge he said there was a train but felt it was quite a ways away and that we should be able to get across the bridge in time. Well, we had trouble getting the car on the tracks, and we were only about halfway across the bridge when I heard the whistle of the train and could see the black smoke from the locomotive rising around the bend in the track. I was nervous! Dogs have better ears than humans. I gave my warning bark and moved to the edge of the car in case I had to jump for safety. The river below didn't look very inviting, but I would rather take a leaping dive than meet the front of a speeding train.

Fortunately, we were able to get off the tracks just as the train rounded the bend. My stomach was twisted in knots after the close call at the train bridge, so I chose to hop off and trot beside the car for a while. This allowed me to work off some of that nervous energy.

Chapter 14

To the Mississippi River

July 9th, 1903

News of our trip was spreading. When we approached towns, Jackson continued his tradition of honking that big bulb horn. I wish he would have stopped that…. It hurt my ears! Crowds of people now lined the streets wanting to see us. If towns were close together, we would go buzzing right on through some of them because Jackson was feeling we were behind schedule.

As we zipped into Columbus, Nebraska, a horse and carriage suddenly turned in front of us. Jackson tried to stop the car, but it was too late. I dropped to the floor just before we made impact. Fortunately, Jackson had been able to slow down the motor car, so the collision with the horse and carriage was fairly minor. Jackson began arguing with the driver of the horse; Crocker started checking to see if there was any damage to the car, and I took my position on the front of the car with a growl to show I was going to protect Jackson. My growl and presence on the front of the car must have made a difference as the man driving the horse and carriage calmed down, and after a few minutes, we were back on our way.

Jackson seemed to feel pressure to keep moving. He had recently heard someone else had also started a trip across the country, and he felt our breakdowns had delayed us. We had no routine, no set time for meals, and no set time to make camp for the night. Sometimes I would get hungry or thirsty waiting to stop. Driving late into the night was not uncommon, but for some reason Jackson chose to drive through the night, and we arrived in Omaha, Nebraska the next morning. I was exhausted! Not only did I stay up all night, but trying to watch, listen, and smell for dangers in the dark of night is much more difficult.

July 12th, 1903

A huge crowd greeted us as we came into town. I was so tired! I jumped down from the motorcar, shook the dust off my back, and settled in a safe place between the back wheels for a long nap. While Jackson entertained the crowd for quite some time and had interviews with newspaper reporters, Crocker started working on the car making repairs. I only awoke when Crocker accidently dropped a wrench that landed on my front paw. I jumped awake with a yelp! Seeing that I'm a forgiving dog, I picked up the wrench in my mouth and delivered it back to him. He gave me a gentle pat as a way of saying I'm sorry and thank you. I returned to my nap under the car, only this time a little further back in case another wrench fell.

We started again the next morning in a drizzly rain. The goggles on my face helped keep the raindrops out of my eyes but fogged up so I could not see anything within an hour of leaving town. Crocker took them off for me while Jackson continued to drive. He leaned over and dried my face before putting them back on my head. That was better! I was thankful that Crocker sometimes understood my problems.

Over the next few days we spent a lot of time driving and covered a lot of miles. We stopped at a few small towns along the way for supplies, small repairs, or for Jackson to talk with newspaper reporters. As was my custom, I stayed under the car and napped on these short delays. The flat land of Nebraska had changed to gentle rolling hills as we traveled across Iowa although nothing as steep as the mountains. I enjoyed being able to again see long distances as we crested each ridge.

As we descended a steep hill toward Clinton, Iowa, I noticed it was a busier town than most we had passed through. There were more trees than we had seen since we left the Rocky Mountains, a pleasant change of scenery after the open plains. My bigger surprise was the huge river that lay before us, much bigger than any we had yet crossed. I had never seen so much water. I had no idea how we would ever cross that! I looked for the train bridge and quickly realized it was too busy to cross safely. I hoped Jackson had a better plan.

Jackson brought the car to a stop, and as usual, a crowd began to gather around us. I hopped down and was just about to settle under the car for my customary nap when a young collie about my age came up to the car. His name was Sparky. He had a playful personality, and soon we left the crowd that had gathered around the Vermont and were playing a game of chase. I picked up a stick, and he tried to get it from me. I then dropped it, and he picked it up and tried to keep it from me. I enjoyed the exercise, but it made me miss my brothers and sisters from when I was a pup.

I heard Jackson whistle for me. It had been much too short of a visit, but

I let out a soft "woof" to say goodbye to my new friend and went bounding back to the car. Taking my place in the front of the car, I saw Sparky one last time as Jackson steered the car onto a small boat he called a ferry. I gathered from Jackson's and Crocker's conversation that this huge river was the Mississippi River. Jackson was thrilled to be crossing it as he felt this symbolically meant we had crossed the halfway point of our journey.

Chapter 15

Chicago and Beyond

July 13th, 1903

Once on the other side of the
Mississippi River, it was a sprint to
Chicago. The roads were becoming
better, and we were able to travel
faster and further now that we no
longer had to deal with mud holes.
Farms now lined the roads, replacing
the grasslands we had recently traveled
through. New smells were tickling my
nose, and occasionally a stray dog
would start to chase us. As much as I
wanted to play with another of my kind,
I chose not to as I also took my job
seriously and did not want anything to
happen to Jackson, Crocker, or the
motor car affectionately called the
Vermont. Besides, if I had gotten off the
car to play, it might have slowed down
our journey, or worse, I could have
been left behind.

July 17th, 1903

As we approached Chicago, we met more travelers on the roads; most of them were traveling by horse and wagons, but some were on bicycles. The buildings were starting to squeeze close to the road and were as tall as the cliffs we encountered in the mountains. It felt like we were between the canyons we had traveled through just weeks before, only now the roads were much smoother and they were packed with people, horses, carriages, bicycles, and the occasional motor car. I had never seen so many people in my short life. It was all strange to me. The road hazards of boulders and washouts had changed to horses pulling wagons and bicycles darting in and out of any available space.

Despite the better roads, Jackson drove slower. He didn't want to repeat the accident we had with the horse and wagon in Nebraska, and who could tell where these crazy people on bicycles would go next. My head was spinning with excitement from all the people, all the buildings, all the new sounds, and all the new smells.

When we came to a stop in the middle of the city, we were welcomed by all sorts of important people. There were several other cars running around on the streets that were similar to the Vermont. However, our car stood out from these shiny vehicles because of the layers of mud and sacks of supplies that buried the car.

Jackson and Crocker were being treated as really important people. I even had to sit still while some people from the newspaper took my picture. While Jackson and Crocker were distracted with all the excitement, I had become distracted by my nose. I smelled some good sausage being cooked somewhere down the street, and my stomach told me to go investigate. Who knew when I might eat again, so I obeyed my stomach and followed my nose.

Around the corner I quickly found the little shop that was making the sausage, but the door was closed and no one was there to open it. I jumped up and put my paws on the dirty panes of glass as I looked through the window. A young woman inside saw me and came out with a few scraps of meat in a wood bowl. A moment later an old man with a mustache came out, scolded the young woman for feeding me, and chased me off with a broom. I figured I wasn't welcome for a second helping. I guess the layers of dust and mud caked on my fur made me look a bit like a wandering mutt.

Looking back towards where I left Jackson and Crocker with the Vermont, I saw the large crowd was still gathered. There was no sense trying to wiggle through that forest of legs, so I decided I would take a tour of the city. The numerous new smells were overwhelming; some were delicious, and some were repulsive. No one seemed too concerned with me as I trotted along. I saw some other dogs and went to introduce myself, but they were on leashes, and their owners quickly shooed me away.

After a short tour of the city, I decided it might be wise to head back. Yikes, where was I? For a moment I panicked as I realized how careless I had been in my wandering. I told myself to relax and trust my nose. Sniffing for my own scent and the trail I had left was a bigger challenge than I thought it would be, because the smell of myself interfered with the scent of where I'd been. I also had to block out the thousands of other scents that were being left. There were a few times I lost my bearings, but thankfully a small gust of wind brought me the familiar smells of Jackson and Crocker. I followed my nose in that direction to find the crowd had gotten a little smaller. I was able to easily weave in out of the forest of legs and plopped down under the car for a long nap. Despite all the new excitement, I was tired.

I must have been dog tired. I awoke to a little rat sniffing by my ear.

I jumped up with a snarl, and the little critter scampered off into the darkness. The city was now much quieter; there was no one around the car. It was dark with an exception of the street lamps that flickered and glowed every hundred feet. I had no idea where Jackson and Crocker had gone, but I thought I should continue to stand guard by the car. I checked the food supply to make sure no other rats were making themselves a midnight snack and then slept the rest of the night with one ear perked up and alert.

As morning dawned, the city began to take on new life again. Several cars came puttering up to the hotel and parked near the Vermont. Jackson and Crocker showed up a little later and were preparing to leave. In all the excitement they had forgotten to feed me and paid no attention to my whines for food. I guess finding breakfast was up to me. I trotted out from under the car hoping the kind young woman from yesterday might again be at the shop around the corner with more meat scraps. I could always hope!

I again hopped up with my paws on the window. No luck! The man with the broom came after me, yelling something in a language I did not understand. I scampered away only to have two young men start to chase me. Hey now, it might have been before breakfast, but I am always ready for a game of chase.

Soon I had quite a following with several people chasing me. Some were dressed up in nice clothes; some had goggles like Jackson and Crocker wore. At about that moment, Crocker came dashing after me…. I couldn't stop, I was having too much fun as I weaved between carriages and bicycles on the streets. A few minutes later I heard Jackson's whistle. I looked up to see him holding a sausage. Now that looked like the breakfast I was looking for. So I ran up to him and politely sat at his feet. He gave me the sausage and then tied a rope to my collar to keep me from leaving again. I guess he had been ready to start traveling when I went looking for breakfast.

Back at the car, Jackson gave me another piece of sausage and put my goggles on before hoisting and tying me into the car. I tried to tell him that now that I had food in my stomach, he did not need to worry about me jumping from the car. Why can't people understand dogs? Crocker gave the handle on the side of the car a crank to start the motor and soon the Vermont was idling noisily along the side of the street. Many other cars had joined the Vermont parked along the street to give us a big send off. I took my place with my paws on the dashboard as Jackson gave the horn a honk and once again we started on our journey, but this time we led a parade of cars as we snaked out of the city.

By the time darkness descended on us we had made it to South Bend, Indiana. The next day we were on our way to Toledo, Ohio. Of course the weather did not improve as the rains continued and the roads were still muddy, but nothing as bad as the "Buffalo Wallows" we encountered earlier. The Vermont continued to splash along.

Chapter 16

Car Parade

July 20th, 1903

Before Chicago, we saw very few cars on the whole journey. Now I was seeing them more often, but even I was surprised as we approached Cleveland. I was at my lookout perch with my paws on the dash when I noticed another parade of cars coming toward us. There were more than twenty cars! If you see a dog gently bobbing and turning its head slightly, that means we are counting. The herding dogs back in Idaho taught me how to count. Because they are always counting livestock and thought every dog should know how to count. I must admit, it is a pretty good skill to know.

The people in the parade of cars signaled to Jackson to stop the car. I gave my warning growl as they approached us. It turned out that among the group was one of the important people in the Winton Company, the company that made the Vermont, and he wanted to greet Jackson and Crocker. A bunch of reporters with cameras got out, blocking the whole road as Jackson and Mr. Shanks shook hands. I think it was the longest handshake in history! The cameras were all clicking; and reporters were yelling out to do it again. People have weird ways of greeting each other. Dogs keep it simple. You walk up to another dog, sniff noses, then step to the right and sniff their hind end. In five seconds you know if you've met a friend or a troublemaker.

After the longest handshake in history, Mr. Shanks, of the Winton Company, led us and the rest of the cars in another parade toward Cleveland. People were lined up along the side of the road waving and cheering for us. Being so concerned about security, my ears were always on alert, and the constant honks and toots that came from all the cars started to drive me crazy.

The parade stopped in front of
the Hollenden Hotel. Whenever we
stopped, I usually jumped off and got
under the car to take a nap to avoid the
crowds that gathered. However, this big
crowd didn't give me room to jump, so I
stayed on board. The crowd slowly
drifted into the hotel taking Jackson and
Crocker with them. I knew that meant I
was left in charge of guarding the
Vermont from newsboys who got a little
too close or panhandlers trying to snag
something from under the tarp on the
back of the car. Being a bulldog, a
simple growl took care of most
problems. It is not that I wanted to be
unfriendly, but hey, if it isn't yours,
then keep your paws off!

Later that evening, Crocker came
and released the car to some mechanics
who would do repairs on it overnight. I
don't think Crocker wanted me to tour
this city as I did in Chicago because he
took me with him back into the hotel. It
was strange that the hotel staff
welcomed me, as usually they don't
want a dirty dusty dog leaving paw
prints on their beautiful carpets. I found

it rather odd that Crocker also grabbed my goggles. He put my goggles on my face and brought me to Jackson. We were then directed to sit down while somebody fussed over which direction I was looking, then fussed over a wrinkle in Jackson's coat and then finally took a picture. WOW! There was a flash like lightning, but there was no boom of thunder. The flash of light came from the camera bulb and was startling. In the outdoors the flash bulb isn't a big deal, but inside a dim room, it hurts the eyes! The next morning we were on the front page of the newspaper.

Chapter 17

The Accident

July 23rd, 1903

The next day I was glad to be out of the big city and on the road again. Even though we were sloshing through mud and being drenched by rainstorms, it was more enjoyable than weaving through a thousand legs at a reception with people more interested in the car than a dog.

According to Jackson, the most direct route would be to attempt to cross the Appalachian Mountains. Jackson decided, however, we already had enough of mountains and redirected us along a slightly longer route through New York to avoid them. Instead of traveling roads next to the railroad, we now traveled roads that ran beside the Erie Canal. I howled my greetings as we sped past dogs that were lazily riding the canal boats being gently pulled by a steady horse or mule. When we stopped to refuel, I met one of the canal dogs. His life sounded boring compared to mine. Like me, his job was security, but his job was slow and boring as he went along the same route every day with a top speed a turtle could match.

I could sense the excitement in Jackson and Crocker. There were less complaints about the roads and their excitement was growing each day as we were getting closer to New York City. Crowds of people began to line the roads near towns cheering us on. I guess the news reporters had spread the story of our journey.

Crocker lit the big light on the front of the car as we continued driving late into the night. The condition of the roads improved, so Jackson increased our speed despite the darkness that loomed around us. Once again I had taken my place with my paws on the dashboard as the wind whistled past my ears. My goggles were a bit smudged with mud so my forward vision was not as clear as it should have been. BAM! I cartwheeled up in the air! As I twisted in the air to get my feet below me for landing, I saw in the corner of my eye that Jackson and Crocker were also flying head over heels. The car had hit some obstacle that none of us had seen, launched itself into the air and spilled each of us onto the ground before crashing into some brush in the ditch. I didn't quite get my legs under me before landing, and neither did Jackson or Crocker. They laid on the side of the road for a few moments, looking rather stunned.

I quickly regathered my wits and went and licked Jackson's face. I find licking a person's face will immediately tell you if they are OK. Jackson was not seriously hurt as he immediately pushed me away and got to a kneeling position. Crocker had sat up by this time and was struggling to his feet. All of us were stunned at how quickly our accident had happened. Jackson, being a doctor, checked himself and Crocker over before checking on me. I was licking my right front paw, maybe a small sprain, but it wasn't too bad.

Crocker then started checking over the Vermont which had continued down the road another 50 yards before crashing into some brush in a ditch. The motor was still idling as if nothing had happened. Other than the fenders being ripped off, there was no major damage to the Vermont. We resumed our places and traveled a bit slower, passing through several towns before stopping for the night in Little Falls, New York.

Chapter 18

Meeting Bertha

July 25th, 1903

The next morning we found the skies had finally cleared for the first time in weeks. Jackson looked over the maps as Crocker inspected the car for fuel, water, oil and to make sure nothing more was broken on the car after our accident the night before. I think some parts of the car had been held on by the mud that encased it which was as hard as cement.

Jackson was anxious to get started, but I still did not have my goggles on. I had learned to sit up on just my rear legs and brush my front paws across my face as a signal to Jackson and Crocker to put the goggles on. After getting my goggles situated over my eyes, I quickly leapt up on the car and took my place in the center, much to the enjoyment of spectators who came to see us off on our journey.

Once again we zoomed along a dusty road that ran beside the Erie Canal, barely pausing as we zipped through little towns. Sometimes we were slowed by horse or mule team towing a canal boat, but the dryer weather and better roads made it much easier to travel.

Arriving in Albany, New York, Jackson was trembling with excitement. At first I thought perhaps he was becoming ill, but hearing the energy in his voice as he spoke with the flood of reporters that greeted us made me realize he was very excited. Instead of calling it a day and staying for the night, Jackson and Crocker decided we would drive through the night. Crocker inspected the big headlight in the center of the front of the car and added some kerosene to the side lamps as Jackson cut short his interviews with reporters.

We now followed the Hudson River on the Albany Post Road. The small towns on our journey were lined with crowds who cheered us on. The daylight faded to starlight with the big headlight guiding our way. As we pulled into Peekskill, New York, I heard a hissing sound coming from the front of the car. I sounded my warning bark to alert Jackson and Crocker that something was wrong. They looked at me, patted my head and told me everything was alright. Well, two minutes later the sound changed to a thump, thump, and the car started drifting to the right. We had a flat tire. Stopping in front of a hotel, I thought we were stopping for the night. Nope. Crocker was going to fix the tire that just went flat, and we were going to continue on through the darkness. I hopped down and took my usual place under the car where I was safe from being stepped on.

After the long day of travel, I was peacefully dozing off for a light nap when I sensed a group of several cars quickly approaching us. A well-dressed lady jumped out of the first car, lifted her skirts and started running toward us calling out "Horatio". I sprang up and gave a deep throated growl to warn the approaching visitors that I would protect Jackson and Crocker. At that moment Jackson lost all his senses. He jumped up from where he was helping Crocker, called out "Bertha" and ran to the lady who had called out his name. I took off after him, barking a warning that we did not know these people. His arms were spread wide, like a bird trying to fly, as he embraced this well dressed lady.

The next few minutes were very confusing. There was crying, laughter, kissing, hugging, and excited voices filling the dark quiet street. I had never seen Jackson behave like this, so I tried to get in the middle of this gathering by barking and growling my warnings to these intruders. Jackson was telling me to settle down when Crocker grabbed my collar and pulled me back while telling me it was OK. How could it be OK with Jackson behaving like this? He had lost his mind.

I soon learned that the well-dressed lady was Jackson's wife,

Bertha. He had talked about her and written many letters to her, but this was the first time I had met her. If Jackson accepted her, then I would too. I tentatively went up to her and sniffed her skirt, and she stooped down and extended her hand. I sniffed it and then gave it a gentle lick letting her know I was her friend. Jackson told her to scratch me between the ears, and I would be her friend forever. He was right about that!

With Bertha now at his side, Jackson greeted the other members of the group which included important people from the Winton Company, who made our car, as well as reporters. Once I realized there was no need to be alarmed, I trotted back to the Vermont and tried to doze off while Crocker finished fixing the flat tire. A couple people from the group came and hung a banner on the side of the car which stated "First Across the Continent - San Francisco to New York." Since the Vermont was getting so much attention, I decided one of the other vehicles might be a quieter place to snooze. I saw one that looked just like the Vermont, except it didn't have nearly as much mud on it. I pawed at the ground, walked in two circles under the car and settled down for some more shut eye.

I had been lightly dozing for a while when I heard Jackson give his shrill whistle and the command for me to jump up in the car. Being awakened with such little sleep, I drug myself to my feet and jumped up into the car. The next few moments brought a lot of confusion. First, the legs in that car did not smell or look like Jackson's and Crocker's legs. Secondly, the resulting surprise of the people attached to those legs caused a bit of panicked shouts followed by deep laughs. I had jumped into the wrong car. Jackson hollered at me to come, but I was confused. He had just told me to get up. I was on the motor car where I was supposed to be. Jackson finally came and got me out and restored me back to my place in the Vermont. I was relieved to be with my people and in my motor car.

Chapter 19

New York and the Finish

July 26th, 1903

Once we were all sorted out, we led the small parade of cars into the night destined for New York City. Jackson was determined to finish this journey tonight.

Similar to Chicago, the buildings started to enclose the streets like the canyons we encountered out west. At 4:30 in the morning, a nearly deserted Fifth Avenue was awakened as Jackson, for the final time, honked the horn of the Vermont to announce our arrival in New York City. I had by now become accustomed to the honk of the horn. One of the members of the parade that escorted us the last few miles into New York City attached small American flags to the Vermont in recognition of crossing the continent.

Being so early in the morning there was no crowd, just the sleepy night porter at the Holland House Hotel as the small welcoming parade rattled down Fifth Avenue. The trip had taken Jackson and Crocker 63 days, 12 hours, and 30 minutes from their starting point in San Francisco. Although I had not been with them from the start, I had traveled the last 43 days and crossed most of North America with them. I had experienced sandy deserts and towering mountains; storms and blazing sun; vast grasslands and bustling cities. Now the journey was coming to an end; what would tomorrow be like? I could wait for the answers, as right now, I just wanted a quiet place to lay my head on my paws.

The crowds came as the day progressed, and for the next four days the car was on display for all those who were curious to come see. At first, I entertained all the reporters who insisted on taking pictures of me wearing my goggles as I sat on the car. It was no fun in the hot city, but a dog has to do what a dog has to do.

During the next few days my life began to change. On July 30th, Jackson again loaded up the Vermont. Crocker said good bye and scratched me one last time between my ears, and then adjusted my googles like he had so many times before. I did not know that he would not be traveling with us anymore. I jumped aboard to my usual place and Bertha, Jackson's wife, sat in Crocker's seat for the ride to Jackson's home. I whined and tried to push her out with my nose, but Crocker reached across her and gently grabbed my head with both hands. He rubbed the sides of my face and told me it was okay and that his job was done. I didn't know what he meant at first, but that was the last time I saw Crocker.

The trip to Jackson's home in Burlington, Vermont took a week. There were more breakdowns, but now Jackson did all the repairs on his own from what he had learned from Crocker. Bertha watched in amazement at the patience and skills Jackson had learned over the past several weeks.

Jackson had completed his historic journey. No longer would I perch on the dashboard for hours on end scanning the horizon. No more naps under the car as it was being repaired. No more chasing prairie dogs or jack rabbits, although I did find squirrels at Jackson's home in Vermont to be a good challenge.

Every once in awhile I would get the itch to take a ride. I would retrieve my googles and drop them at Jackson's feet. Jackson must have felt the same as he would get the "Vermont" out of the carriage house and take me for a ride in the country. Like old times, I whined and rubbed my face until he put my googles on. I would then jump back to my place with my paws on the dashboard, hoping we might be off on another adventure.

Over the next few years, motor cars became much more common. Other dogs would get excited and bark wildly while chasing the cars down the road. I watched them hurry by from my new perch on the porch of Jackson's home in Vermont as I thought back to all the adventures I had crossed the country with Jackson. There was no need for me to join the other dogs in the chase to prove my status. I had been the first dog to cross the continent by car; nobody could take the pride I felt away from me.

Author's Note

The story about Bud is based on a true story. Horatio Nelson Jackson was the first person to cross America in an automobile in 1903 with the assistance of his mechanic, Sewall Crocker. In Idaho, Jackson picked up a bulldog he affectionately named Bud, who became the mascot of the journey. Many of the events that Bud shares in the story are largely based on accounts of Jackson's journal which can be read in the book *Horatio's Drive*.

In writing this story from Bud's perspective, I had to add details that might happen to a dog that would not have been part of Horatio Jackson's journal. I used observations of my dogs over the years, and the mischief they would get into, to give Bud a story to tell.

The car in the story was a 1903 Winton, a company that is no longer in business. Jackson nicknamed the car the "Vermont" in honor of the state where he lived. The actual car that made the journey still exists and is part of an exhibit at the Smithsonian

Institution, a series of museums in Washington DC. The exhibit also includes a cast statue of Bud, complete with goggles.

The route of their journey across America also has significance. In 1903, there was not a system of roads for automobiles that traveled from one coast to the other. The roads that did exist connected larger towns but were not well maintained and did not connect across the country. The first road to cross America, called the Lincoln Highway, was completed in 1913 and closely followed the route that Jackson and Crocker traveled in 1903. This road now follows portions of Interstate 80 and US Highway 30.

We do not know what happened to Bud after his cross country journey. I feel it would be safe to say that he lived out his life in Vermont at the home of Horatio Nelson Jackson, with whom he traveled across America.

Other Books by Arthur Brood

It's 1912, Henry and his brother Robert are fascinated by the automobile. Their father calls the automobile a noisy, smelly contraption. When the mud hole near their farm continues to trap automobiles, their father gives the boys the responsibility of using the horse to pull stuck automobiles from the mud. One adventure leads to another, but when the mischief goes too far, what will happen to their summer plans?

Through it all, Henry learns that honesty is more important than money, and a job well done sometimes has its rewards.

Available at Amazon.com

Other Books by Arthur Brood

In the fall of 1912, eleven year old Henry is disappointed when an early snowfall threatens to keep the Model T parked in the barn for the winter. Known for his crazy ideas, Henry finds a way to keep the car out of the barn and himself behind the wheel. When an outbreak of influenza strikes the town, Henry and his "snow car" are put to the test.

Will Henry's crazy ideas get him into more mischief, or give him the chance to show responsibility and courage?

Available at Amazon.com